W9-BSO-245

by Ben H. Winters
illustrated by Adam F. Watkins

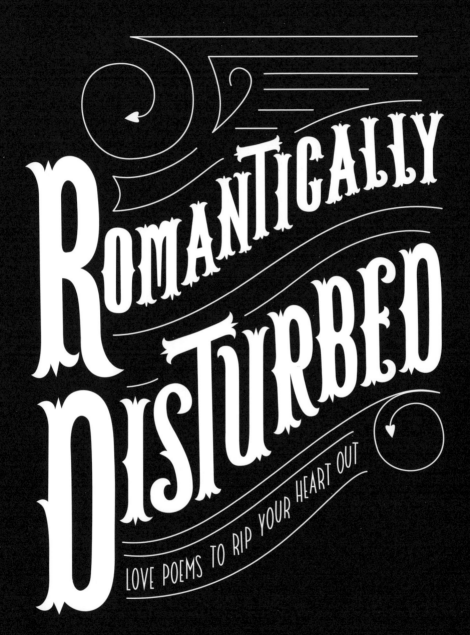

ROMANTICALLY DISTURBED

LOVE POEMS TO RIP YOUR HEART OUT

PRICE STERN SLOAN
Penguin Young Readers Group
An Imprint of Penguin Random House LLC

Text copyright © 2015 by Penguin Random House LLC. Illustrations copyright © 2015 by Adam F. Watkins. All rights reserved.
Published by Price Stern Sloan, an imprint of Penguin Random House LLC, 345 Hudson Street, New York, New York 10014.
PSS! is a registered trademark of Penguin Random House LLC. Manufactured in China.

Library of Congress Cataloging-in-Publication Data is available.

ISBN 978-0-8431-7313-0   10 9 8 7 6 5 4 3 2 1

by Ben H. Winters
illustrated by Adam F. Watkins

ROMANTICALLY
DISTURBED

LOVE POEMS TO RIP YOUR HEART OUT

PSS!
PRICE STERN SLOAN
An Imprint of Penguin Random House

LOVE IS A MONSTER #1
(LOVE IS A GHOST)

Hovering in the shadows
in the corners of your mind.
Reminding you of feelings
you'd prefer to leave behind.

It flickers—disappears—
is it over?
Hard to say.
But you *think* it's gone away.
It's done!
It's through!
You think you're safe
and then—
BOO!

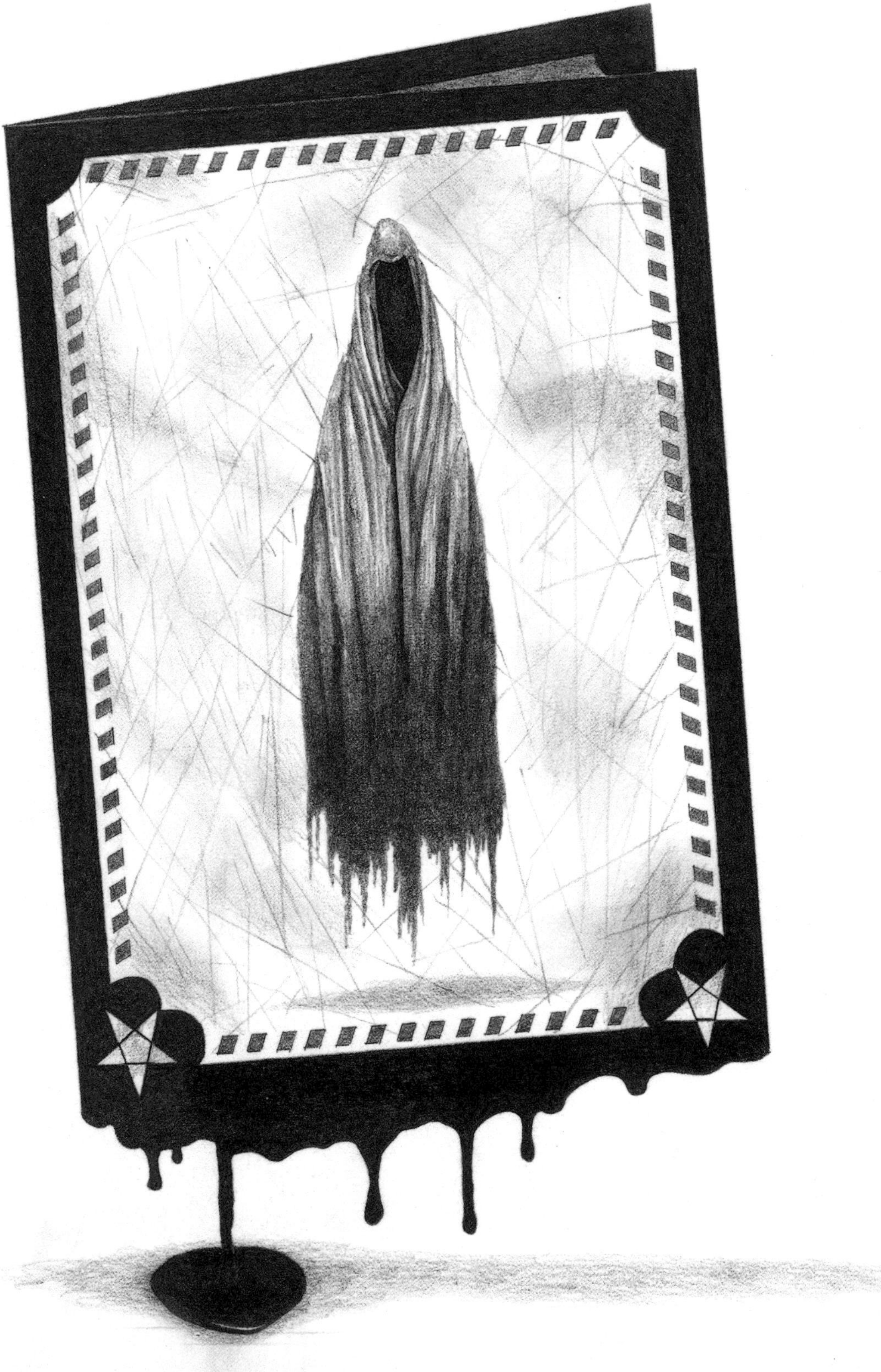

THE FORTUNE-TELLER

I held my palm up to old Madame Dupree
and said, "Oh, wise woman! Describe what you see!"

She started with what she called the life line.
She looked good and hard, and said, "This looks fine."

Next the line for career—
she said, "No trouble here."
Then a line she called "fate"
said, "Okay, this is great."

Then came the love line, and "Gee—but—"
"What?" I said, "Hey! Answer me—
what?"

She just trembled and stared,
looking more and more scared.
She muttered, "My God,"
said, "This line's a bit . . . odd.
'Cause it's got this funny bulge,
and it makes this odd shelf,
and you see where it zigs and bends back on itself?
Then it makes these strange circles, like knots in old wood.
I don't know what it means, child,
but I know it ain't good."

VARIATION ON A THEME

Shall I compare thee to a summer's day?
In truth you more remind me of a hurricane.
Your mood transforming from sky blue to gray,
the thunder in your voice, your tears like rain.
When the clouds come rolling in, I start preparing,
before your smile's eclipsed and dark descends.
You know, now that I'm all done with comparing—
I think perhaps we're better off as friends.

CLASSIC STORY

Boy meets girl.
Girl likes boy.
Out to dinner.
Both enjoy.
Moonlight walk,
skipping stones.
Boy turns into enormous multi-mouthed monster,
teeth like razors,
eyes shoot lasers.
Eats girl up,
spits out bones.

THE BOY I USED TO LIKE

There's a boy I used to like,
but he fell for someone new.
I cried and cried and cried,
you know, like people do.
But then I got myself together,
and now I wear a smile.
I hardly think of him these days—
plus no one's seen him for a while.

LOVE POTIONS

Go ahead,
brew that brew.
Fix that potion.
Stew that stew.
But, buddy,
please,
before you do—
just take good care—
I *beg* of you.

'Cause this drink you think will turn her head
might make it spin around instead,
might make her eyes glow green and red,
might make her float above her bed.

So go ahead and brew that brew.
Fix that nice hot magic stew.
Just keep in mind
that when you do,
it might not go how you want it to.

LOVE IS A MONSTER #2
(LOVE IS FRANKENSTEIN'S MONSTER)

A beast assembled from other parts,
all stitched and bolted together.
It shouldn't exist, and it's frightening!

Friendship, attraction, confusion, two hearts,
and then the perfect weather
for that single zap of lightning.

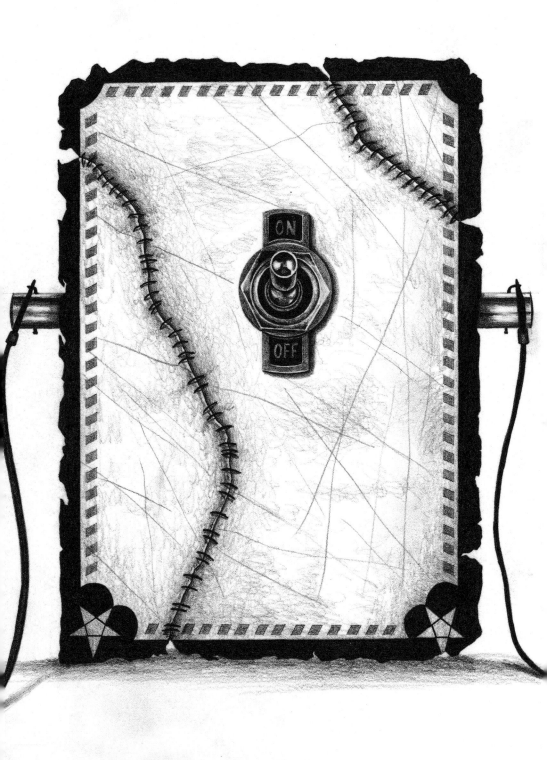

HOW TO PICK
THE PERFECT GIFT

Candy's too sweet.
Jewelry gets rusted.
Flowers will wilt.
A music box can be busted.
I'm taking all this junk back where I bought it,
'cause now I've found the perfect gift—
just don't ask me where I got it.

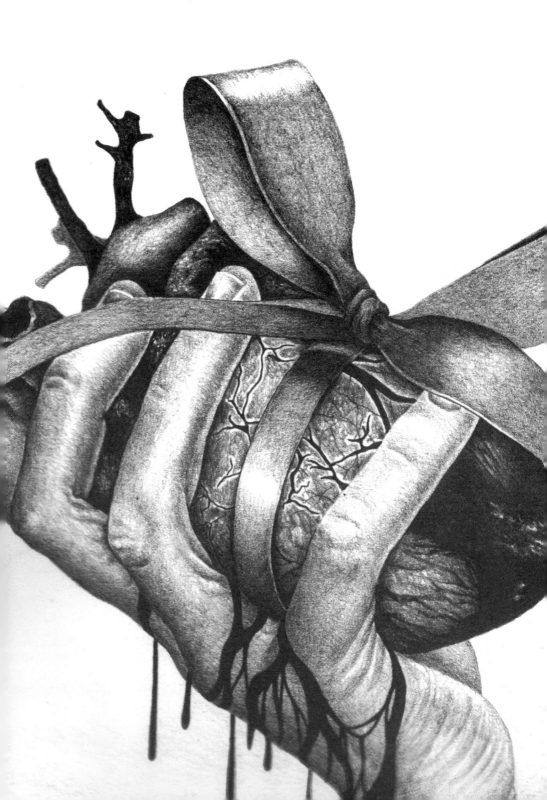

THERE ARE LIMITS

Yes, of course,
you shouldn't be shallow.
Real love's what remains
when looks and youth are long gone.

I know these things are true.
I try not to be shallow, I do.

. . . But come *on.*

YOU MAKE ME FEEL

When you smile,
I get sick.
The room spins.
My tongue is thick.
My ears get red.
I trip and stumble.
I lose my head.
I mutter and mumble.
I can't think or talk or move,
no matter how hard I try.
So, wait, do I love you?
Or am I about to die?

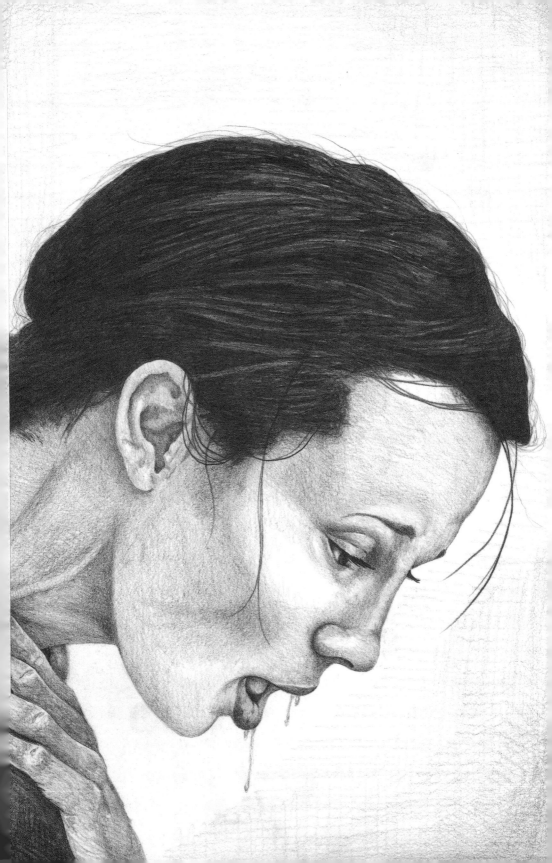

THE GIRL WHO KISSED
A FROG

Once upon a long ago,
in a far and distant land,
a lonely princess was longing so
for a prince to take her hand.

And then, upon a summer's day,
down by the royal brook,
she saw a frog (or so they say),
with a royal kind of look.

And sad to say, that royal miss
has not been herself since.
She gave that frog a dainty kiss,
but it was definitely NOT a prince.

LOVE IS A MONSTER #3
(LOVE IS A DEMON)

You feel you've changed, and that is true.
There's something there inside of you.
You're a host.
You've got a guest,
a pal,
a parasite,
a pest.

Good luck, poor soul. You're possessed.

A VERY UNUSUAL CANDY BOX

A very unusual candy box
with sweet treasures hidden inside:
Instead of nougat,
there's arsenic.
No caramel,
only cyanide.
This one's got tacks!
And this one has nails!
There's broken glass in *here*!
A dusting of gravel,
a drizzle of blood,
and it's all for you, my dear.

ZOMBIES: BASIC ADVICE

If a zombie should fall in love with you,
don't rush it! Take it slow.
And if he says, "I want to hold your hand"—
say no.

CUPID

I don't care for him, myself,
the horrid little buzzing elf
who aims his nasty bow
at us poor saps below.
A hideous gremlin, up above,
laughing as we fall in love.
You! With her! Go on, do it!
You! With him! That's right—get to it!
And off he flies, cackling still.
Better he should shoot to kill.

LOVE IS A MONSTER #4

(LOVE IS A VAMPIRE)

One night.
One bite.
In sink the teeth.

And boom,
it's doom
for you.

It's in
your skin,
and the flesh beneath.
You're caught,
you're got,
you're through.

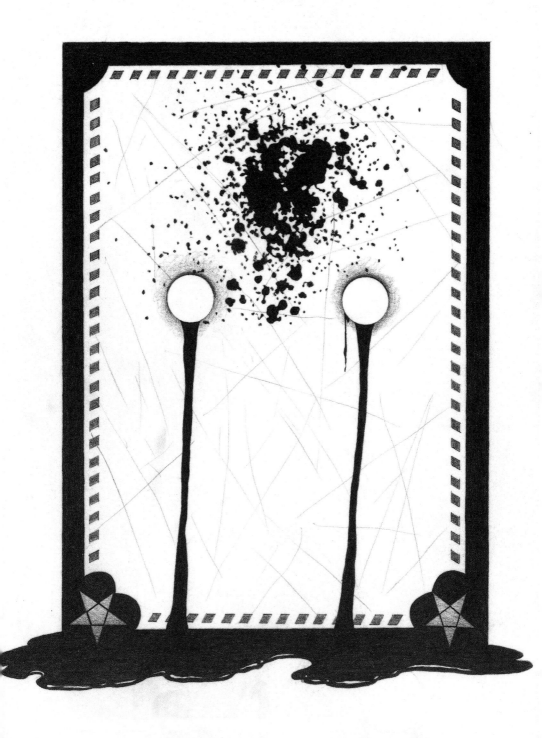

WHAT HAPPENED TO MY FRIEND JAY?

We were pirates.
We read books.
We played cops.
We caught crooks.

Now he's grinning and holding her hand,
the buffoon!
Now he spends his allowance
on flowers, the loon.

He says it's love, and it's changed his soul.
I suspect alien mind control.

PERFECT COUPLE

He's got six eyes.
She's got four.
He's got twelve arms.
She's got more.
He's got just one tooth, as long as a sword.
She's got a head
like an overripe gourd.
She's got nasty yellow teeth.
He's got purple hair.
Each alone is horrifying,
but don't they make the perfect pair?

JEALOUS

Lucky ghost, good for you.
The only thing you say is "boo."
You don't spend all day up in your head,
regretting some dumb thing you said.
Lucky zombie, what a guy.
Rotting eyeballs never cry.
You're munching people's torn-off parts,
not nursing your own broken hearts.
Lucky vampire, happy fate!
No more sighing for a date.
If you like someone you chance to see,
one quick bite and you're home free.
You cursed souls
have one sweet deal:
When you're undead, you cannot feel.

ONE WISH

"You get a wish," the genie said, "and I'm *serious,* just one.
Just tell me what it is you want, and boom! It shall be done."
I didn't even blink.
I didn't have to think.
I knew what I wanted to see.
"Jane McGuire, this girl from choir, I want her to fall for me."

"No problem," the genie said, that jerk,
and boy oh boy, did that wish work.
Jane fell down the stairs and landed
on her nose and broke her hand and
her leg and her foot and her head.
And now here she is in this hospital bed.

So now what am I wishing for?
Another wish—just one wish more.

DECISIONS, DECISIONS

Class rule: You give a valentine
to every single kid.
But there's lots of kids that I don't like,
so here is what I did:

Naomi's I dragged through the mud.
Henry's got some snot and blood.
Luke's I put some old mustard on.
Bob's got dog poop from the lawn.

Sending cards is not a crime,
and I can't *wait* for Christmastime!

Happy Valentine's Day!
NAOMI
Happy HENRY Valentine's Day!
Happy LUKE Valentine's Day!
Valentine
BOB

THE GHOST'S REPLY

What, you think you're lonely?
Boo hoo.
Got no special sweetie?
Poor you.
I'm a ghost, and I've been dead
for one hundred sixty years.
I've had no girlfriend since the decade before
the outbreak of the Civil War.
No one to take you to the movies?
So sit home and watch TV.
You might find love tomorrow.
Not me.

THE GIRL WHO LIVED IN THE HAUNTED HOUSE

There's a girl at school with dark eyes,
black hair.
She'd like to be friends.
DON'T YOU DARE.
Her house is the one with the owls in the eaves,
and the fat black crow.
She'd like to have you over.
DON'T GO.

TWO SIDES OF NIGHTTIME

Moonglow on a rose.
Stars shine up above.
Everybody knows
that night's the time for love.

No sun to cast its glow.
Darkness looming large.
The evil spirits know
that night's when they're in charge.

JUST ONE MORE THING
TO TELL HER

He sits in the dark
of his living room.
Every night,
all alone in the gloom,
he mutters and murmurs her name.
It's like a séance!
Or a Ouija board party.
But it's just the old man—
it's no game.

"My darling, my darling,
say something.
My darling, darling,
respond!
I'm waiting to hear
you still love me, my dear,
though you're off
in the Great Beyond.
I'm waiting and calling,
and calling and waiting,
and missing you awfully, my pet."

He just sits in the gloom,
in the dark of that room,
and he hasn't heard anything yet.

A HISTORY LESSON

Saint Valentine, just by the way,
was brutally murdered in Rome in the year 269.
First he was tortured and terribly beaten,
Then beheaded and thrown to wolves to be eaten.
So there's a nice little story
(and sorry so gory)
to include in your next valentine.

LOVE IS A MONSTER #5
(LOVE IS DR. JEKYLL AND MR. HYDE)

The chameleon,
the hidden place,
the mild-mannered fellow
with the secret face.
The shocking truth,
the shadowed heart,
the unseen danger,
the hidden part.

VAMPIRES: BASIC ADVICE

In movies, they're all so good-looking
and charming and raffish and vain.
Vampires in life look like people:
some handsome, some ugly, some plain.
Just remember that if you should see one,
don't kiss him, 'cause then you will *be* one.

THE RING

She said, "My dear, what a gorgeous ring!"
He said, "I know, but there's just one thing—
one thing that you must know."
(She wasn't really listening,
just staring at the sparkling ring,
the glistening, shining, twinkling ring.)
"This ring, it means forever, so—"
"Forever, right, I know, I know."
She slipped it on, it fit just right—
it gripped her pretty finger tight.

When she thinks back to that moonlit night,
the way it cast its shivering light
(and how she wasn't listening,
just staring at it glistening),
she tugs at it just crying, crying,
and pulls at it, just trying, trying—

And the man's long gone,
and the ring gleams on.
"Forever," she said. "Forever, I know—"
And now the ring will not let go.

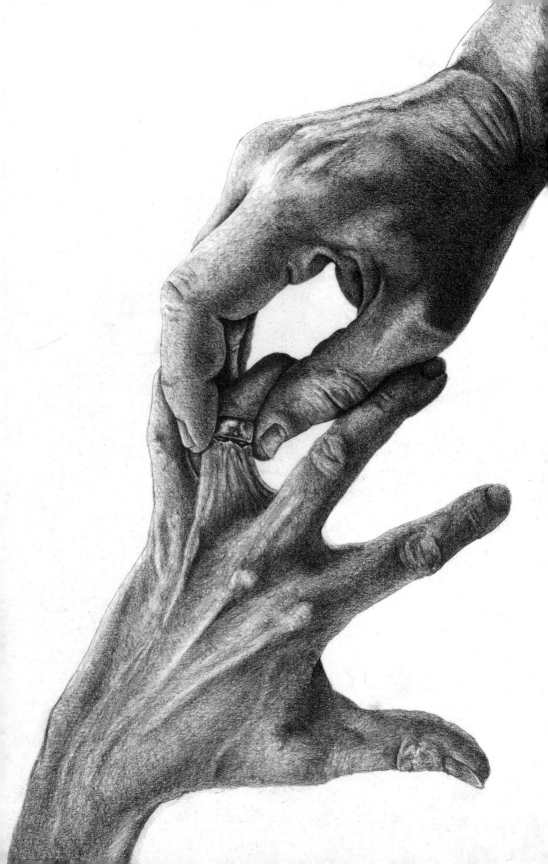

ANOTHER VARIATION ON A THEME

Roses are red,
violets are blue.
All these flowers will die one day;
so will I, and so will you.